STORIES FROM

OLD CHINA

Folklore of the World

Each of the Folklore of the World Books contains carefully selected myths and folktales most representative of a single country. These books will help children to understand people in other lands and will help them to develop an appreciation for their customs and culture. Peace for the world can come only through the spreading of this understanding and appreciation.

The Folklore Books are the third step in the Dolch program, *Steps to a Lifetime Reading Habit.* The series on these graded steps, starting with the most elementary, are: the First Reading Books, the Basic Vocabulary Books, the Folklore Books, and the Pleasure Reading Books.

These Folklore Books are written almost entirely in the Storyteller's Vocabulary, a list of 684 words found by research to be the most useful words in telling stories to young people. This list fits in between that of the Basic Vocabulary Books and that of the Pleasure Reading Books.

Folklore Books are prepared under the direction of Edward W. Dolch, Professor of Education, Emeritus, University of Illinois. In all the series, emphasis is placed on good storytelling and literary quality, as well as on simplicity of vocabulary.

Books in this series are: (to date)

Stories from Alaska	Stories from Mexico
Stories from France	Stories from Spain
Stories from Hawaii	Stories from Old China
Stories from India	Stories from Old Russia
Stories from Italy	Stories from Old Egypt
Stories from Japan	

STORIES FROM

OLD CHINA

Folklore of the World

by EDWARD W. DOLCH
and MARGUERITE P. DOLCH

illustrated by SEONG MOY

GARRARD PUBLISHING COMPANY
CHAMPAIGN, ILLINOIS

j 398.2

Foreword

China is a very, very old country. Long before America was discovered, China was a land of powerful emperors and fierce warriors. There were beautiful cities in China before there were any cities in Europe. These cities grew up around the Emperor and his palace. The Emperor usually built a wall around the city to protect the people from thieves and wild animals.

The people of China believed in many gods. There were gods of war and gods of the home. There were gods that looked after the children. Some gods, such as the dragon, looked like animals. Some dragons were good and brought happiness to people. Some dragons were bad.

Like people all over the world, the Chinese enjoyed telling stories. Because China is such a large country, the stories tell of the ways of the people in many different areas. The story of the water buffalo and the tiger comes from the part of China where these animals are important to the people.

STORIES FROM OLD CHINA brings to the children of today some of the stories that were enjoyed by Chinese children thousands of years ago. After you have read these stories, go to the library and find many other beautiful stories from Old China.

Marguerite P. Dolch
Santa Barbara, California

v

Contents

The Magic Brush

Ma Liang was a little boy who wanted to paint pictures. But he was very poor. Ma Liang had no father and no mother. He could not go to school.

Every day Ma Liang gathered firewood. It was very hard work. At the end of the day Ma Liang was so tired that he often sat down and cried. Sometimes a man would give him a little money for his firewood. Sometimes a woman would give him a bowl of rice.

One day Ma Liang went by the school. He saw the schoolmaster painting a picture with a brush.

"Please give me a brush," said Ma Liang. "I want to paint a picture, too."

"Go away," the schoolmaster said. "You are a poor boy with no father and no mother. You have no money, and you cannot come to my school."

Ma Liang was very sad. He said to himself,

"I know I am a poor boy. But I am going to learn to draw the things I see. I am going to learn to paint pictures."

2

After Ma Liang had gathered his bundle of wood, he sat on the sand. He drew pictures in the sand with his finger. He drew the birds and the fish just right.

When he went to the hut where he slept, he took a piece of wood that had burned black in the fire. He used the wood to draw pictures on the wall of his hut.

Every day Ma Liang looked carefully at everything about him. And every day he drew pictures. Soon the birds he drew looked just like the birds in the trees. The fish he drew looked just like the fish in the river.

Then one night Ma Liang had a dream. An old man said to him,

"Ma Liang, I have brought you a magic brush. Be very careful how you use it."

In the morning, Ma Liang found that he was holding a golden paintbrush in his hand. Then he remembered his dream and what the old man had said.

Ma Liang jumped up and with his magic brush painted a beautiful bird on the wall of the hut. Then right before his eyes the bird became a real bird and flew out of the door. The bird flew into a tree and sang a sweet song.

Ma Liang painted a fine big fish on the wall of his hut. As soon as Ma Liang finished painting the fish it jumped down from the wall.

Ma Liang took the fish to a poor woman who had given him some rice. The woman cooked the fish, and Ma Liang and the poor woman had all that they could eat.

Ma Liang took his magic paintbrush and went from hut to hut in the village. He asked the poor people,

"What is it that you want most of all? Is it something to eat? I will paint it for you."

The poor people laughed at Ma Liang. They said,

"How will your painting a picture help us?"

"Tell me what you want. Then wait and see," said Ma Liang.

Some said that they wanted food. Then Ma Liang would paint rice and fish upon the walls of their hut. Some said that they wanted clothes for their children. Then Ma Liang would paint shoes or dresses. Some said that they wanted a table or a chair.

When Ma Liang finished painting the picture, it would become real.

The poor people of the village were very much surprised. But they were very happy too. There was enough food for everyone. There were enough clothes for everyone. The poor people of the village had everything that they wanted.

Ma Liang was very happy. He painted pictures all day long.

Ma Liang and the Emperor

Ma Liang painted pictures with his magic brush for the poor people of his village. When he finished painting his picture, the picture became real.

Of course, the poor people talked about the boy, Ma Liang, and his wonderful magic brush. Soon the Emperor heard about the boy and sent for him to come to the palace.

The Emperor was not a good man. All he wanted was gold and more gold. He did not look after the people in the villages.

Ma Liang had heard many stories about the Emperor, and he did not like him. But he knew that he had to go with the soldiers to the palace of the Emperor.

The Emperor ordered Ma Liang to paint a golden dragon. But Ma Liang made believe that he did not know what the Emperor said. He took his magic brush and painted an ugly toad. The toad jumped onto the table and into the Emperor's golden rice bowl.

The Emperor was very angry. He took the magic brush away from Ma Liang and said,

"I will paint my own pictures."

The Emperor painted a bar of gold. But the Emperor thought that it was a very small bar. He painted it longer and longer. When he had finished, the bar of gold turned into a giant snake.

The Emperor was afraid. He called his soldiers, and they came and killed the giant snake.

Then the Emperor spoke very kindly to Ma Liang,

"Here is your magic brush. I know that I cannot use it to paint the things I want. But if you will stay in my palace and paint pictures for me, I will make you very rich."

The Emperor ordered Ma Liang to paint a beautiful sea. So he painted a beautiful blue sea.

"There are no fish in the sea," said the Emperor.

Ma Liang painted beautiful golden fish in the sea.

"Paint a big boat for me!" cried the Emperor.

Ma Liang painted a big boat. The Emperor and all his soldiers got on the boat.

Ma Liang painted a big wind. Ma Liang kept on painting the wind. The wind made big waves on the sea. The boat began to fill with water.

"Stop the wind! Stop the wind!" cried the Emperor. "The boat is filling with water."

The wind made so much noise that Ma Liang could not hear the Emperor. Ma Liang kept on painting the wind. The wind got bigger and bigger. The waves got higher and higher.

Soon the big boat and the Emperor and all his soldiers went to the bottom of the beautiful blue sea.

Then Ma Liang said to himself, "The old man in my dream was right. I must be careful how I use this magic brush."

Ma Liang went back to his village. He went among the poor people of his village. When he found a family that needed something very badly he would say,

"My friends, if you will tell no one about my magic brush, I will paint what you need upon the walls of your hut."

And when Ma Liang finished painting the picture, the picture became real.

The poor people of the village had everything that they wanted. They loved Ma Liang and kept his secret.

Sometimes Ma Liang sits in the market place and paints beautiful pictures for the rich people who give him money for his pictures.

Ma Liang does not finish the pictures that he paints in the market place. The birds have no eyes. The fish have no tails. The pictures have to stay on the paper. They cannot become real.

The Water Buffalo and the Tiger

One day a farmer was plowing a field with a water buffalo. The field was very muddy. The water buffalo was pulling the plow very slowly.

"You silly water buffalo," said the farmer. "You move so slowly. Look how quick and strong the tiger is. Why can't you be like the tiger?"

"Why should I be like the tiger?" asked the water buffalo. "I am better than the tiger."

The farmer was angry. He beat the water buffalo with a stick.

"Take me to a tiger," said the water buffalo, "and I will show you that I am better than a tiger."

The next morning the farmer took his water buffalo to a tiger's den. The tiger came out of the den.

The water buffalo shook his sharp horns at the tiger and said,

"Stop! I have not come to fight you today because your teeth are not sharp. Make your teeth very sharp. In three days I will come back and fight you with my horns."

The tiger roared and went back into his den.

"Silly water buffalo, be back in three days and I will kill you," called the tiger. He laughed as he began to make his teeth very sharp.

The tiger sharpened his teeth for three days. He was very angry. No one had ever told him before that his teeth were not sharp enough.

The water buffalo went back to the farm. He sharpened his horns for one day. Then he said to the farmer,

"If you want me to work for you, do as I tell you. Cover my body with straw."

The farmer worked for two days covering his water buffalo with straw. He tied the straw so that the water buffalo had a coat of straw all over his body. Then the water buffalo rolled in the mud. His whole body was covered with a coat of straw and mud.

The water buffalo went to the tiger's den. The tiger came out of his den with a roar. He stopped when he saw the water buffalo.

"Why are you all covered with mud?" asked the tiger.

"It is summer time," said the water buffalo. "You know I take a mud bath every day. The mud keeps me cool in the summer time."

The tiger looked at the water buffalo again.

"You are very fat," said the tiger. Then the tiger laughed. "Today I will have a good dinner of nice fat water buffalo."

"You will not hurt a hair of my body," said the water buffalo.

"I could have killed you three days ago without sharpening my teeth," said the tiger. "And now my teeth are very sharp."

"All right," said the water buffalo. "I will lie down and let you bite me three times. Then you must let me butt you with my horns three times." The water buffalo lay down on the ground.

The tiger laughed and said,

"You are a silly water buffalo."

The tiger rushed at the water buffalo and bit him three times. He was sure the water buffalo was dead. But the tiger could only bite into the straw that covered the water buffalo.

The water buffalo got up and butted the tiger three times with his sharp horns.

The first time the tiger was rolled over on his back. The second time the sharp horns went through the tiger. And the third time the tiger was tossed up into the air and fell back to the ground dead.

The farmer saw that his water buffalo was better than the tiger.

"I shall always be good to my water buffalo even if he does move slowly," said the farmer.

And in China the farmer thinks that the water buffalo is his best friend.

The Kind Dragon

Once upon a time there was a woman who had two sons. The older son worked hard and earned money. But the younger son was just a boy, and he did not know how to earn money.

One day the woman said to the younger son,

"It is time you went out into the world and made your living. Put these pancakes in your pocket and do not come back until you have made your fortune."

The young Boy put the pancakes into his pocket and went out into the world to make his fortune. He was very sad as he walked along the road.

At last he came to a river. He sat down and watched the water and began to eat one of his pancakes. He looked down in the grass and saw a very little snake. The Boy felt sorry for the little snake. It lay on the grass as if it could not move.

The Boy took a little box out of his pocket. He put some grass in the box. Then he carefully put the snake into the box.

"I can sell this little snake for
some money," the Boy thought.

The Boy took good care of his
little snake. Day by day the snake
grew and grew. The boy had to
find a pool of water for the snake.

One day the snake said,

"I have grown so big that I
cannot live in this pool of water
any longer. Carry me down to the
river and put me into the water."

The Boy was very sad. He said
to the snake,

"I thought that I could sell you
for some money. My mother says
that I cannot come home until I
bring her a fortune."

"All right," said the snake. "If it is money you want, I shall see that you get it. Just put me into the river."

The Boy made a big basket and put the snake into it. Then he carried the basket to the river. He put the snake into the river.

As soon as the snake was in the river it became a Golden Dragon. It came to the Boy and said,

"You have been kind to me. I will give you a magic donkey. You will have all the money that you want."

The Boy looked and saw a little donkey right beside him.

As he went down the river the Golden Dragon called to the Boy,

"Just say to the donkey, 'Give me money,' and out of the donkey's mouth will come gold and silver. But remember! Do not tell anyone about this."

The Boy looked at the donkey and said,

"If you are a magic donkey, give me money."

Gold and silver came from the donkey's mouth. The Boy filled his pockets with the money.

The Boy started home with his donkey. Night came, and he stopped at an inn.

The Boy said to the Innkeeper,
"Please feed my donkey, but do
not ask him for any money."

The Innkeeper fed the donkey.
But he kept thinking of what the
Boy had said. He wondered why
he should not ask the donkey for
money. Was the Boy just being
silly? Or was this a magic donkey
that could give a man some money?
So the Innkeeper said,

"Donkey, give me some money."

Out of the mouth of the donkey
came gold and silver.

The Innkeeper hid the magic
donkey. In the morning he gave
the Boy another donkey.

When the Boy and the donkey got home, he said to his mother,

"Now, Mother, I have come home with a fortune. You can have all the money that you want. All I have to do is to say to my magic donkey, 'Give me money.'"

But no money came out of the donkey's mouth.

"You are a silly boy!" cried his mother. "You are trying to make fun of me. Take your donkey and go away from my house!"

The Fortune

The Boy who thought he had made his fortune had been fooled. His mother told him not to come home. So the Boy went right to the river and called to the Golden Dragon.

The Golden Dragon put his head out of the water and said,

"What do you want?"

"Why did you make fun of me? When I took your donkey to my mother, the donkey would give her no money. Now I cannot go home."

"If you don't want the donkey I will give you a tablecloth," said the Golden Dragon. "This tablecloth will feed you whenever you are hungry. But remember! Do not tell anyone about this."

The Boy saw a beautiful tablecloth on the grass.

The Boy said to the tablecloth,

"Give me rice and meat, for I am very hungry."

And there before him the Boy saw the best dishes of rice and meat he had ever seen.

The Boy sat down beside the magic tablecloth. He ate all that he wanted.

The Boy took the tablecloth
and started home. Night came,
and he stayed at the inn. The
Innkeeper was very surprised to
see the Boy again. He was afraid
that the Boy had come for his
donkey. But the Boy only said
that he wanted a room because
he wanted to go to bed.

The Innkeeper took the Boy to
a room. He saw that the Boy had
a tablecloth under his arm.

The Boy put the tablecloth on
a table and said to the Innkeeper,
"Do not let anyone touch my
tablecloth. And do not let anyone
ask it for food."

When the Boy was asleep, the Innkeeper stole the magic table-cloth and put another on the table. In the morning the Boy took the tablecloth and went home. He said to his mother,

"I am bringing home my fortune. Just ask for anything that you would like to eat. My magic tablecloth will give it to you."

"You are the same silly Boy that you have always been," cried his mother.

The Boy put the tablecloth on the table.

"My mother, what would you like to eat?"

"I would like some rice," said his mother.

"Give us some rice and some meat," said the Boy.

But there was no rice or meat upon the table.

The mother was very angry, and she beat the Boy.

"Go away from my house you silly boy. You will not make fun of your mother."

The Boy went to the river and called to the Golden Dragon,

"Why do you make fun of me? My mother beat me and will not let me go home until I make my fortune."

The Golden Dragon put his head out of the water.

"My boy, I will help you one more time. I will give you this old stick. But be very careful how you use it. You must take this stick to the inn. Be sure to say to the Innkeeper, 'Do not say, "wooden stick, beat me."'"

The Boy did not see how an old wooden stick could be his fortune.

But he took the stick from the Golden Dragon and went to the inn. The Innkeeper was very glad to see him.

"The Boy is bringing something magic with him," the Innkeeper said to himself.

The Innkeeper took the Boy to his room. The Boy put the stick down and said to the Innkeeper,

"Do not say, 'wooden stick, beat me.'"

Then the Boy went to sleep.

The Innkeeper came and stole the stick. He was sure the stick was a magic stick and he said to the stick,

"Wooden stick, beat me."

The stick jumped up and began to beat the Innkeeper.

"Stop! Stop!" the Innkeeper cried. But the stick kept on beating him.

The Innkeeper ran about his room. He could find no place to hide. At last he ran to the Boy's room.

"Make your stick stop beating me!" cried the Innkeeper. "I will give back your magic donkey and your magic tablecloth."

At once, the stick stopped beating the Innkeeper.

In the morning the Boy took his stick and his magic donkey and his magic tablecloth and went home.

His mother said to him,

"You silly boy, why have you come home without a fortune?"

"My fortune is my magic donkey and my magic tablecloth. Donkey, give me gold and silver. Tablecloth, give me rice and meat."

The Mother saw gold and silver coming out of the donkey's mouth. She saw meat and rice upon her table.

The mother was so surprised that she could not say a word.

The Cloak of Tiger Skin

There once was a poor man and his wife who had one baby boy. This baby boy did not grow like other babies. In one day he was walking. In another day he was talking. And in one week, he was a big boy.

This big boy ate so much that his father and mother did not know how they were going to get enough to feed him. The boy, whose name was Ku-nan, was always hungry.

"I am strong. I must go and find some work," said Ku-nan.

"Go to the Khan," said the boy's mother. "He can use a big strong boy like you."

Ku-nan started out for the Khan's yurt. On the way, he met a hungry wolf.

Ku-nan seized the wolf by the tail and killed it. Then Ku-nan skinned the wolf and cooked the meat. He ate it and felt better.

Ku-nan walked all day. At night he came to the Khan's yurt. There was a whole roasted cow on the table. Ku-nan ate it all.

"You are to be my servant," said the Khan, "for never have I seen a boy so big and strong."

One day the Khan and his servants went hunting in the forest. They met a tiger. It was the biggest tiger that the Khan had ever seen. The Khan was not very brave. He turned his horse around and rode home.

All the servants but Ku-nan ran away. Ku-nan seized the tiger by the tail. He threw it against a tree and killed it. Then he put the tiger over his shoulder and went back to the yurt.

The Khan was surprised to see Ku-nan with the tiger. He said,

"Make me a coat from that tiger's skin."

Ku-nan took the tiger's skin home to his mother. She made a beautiful coat out of the skin.

When the coat was finished, Ku-nan took it to the Khan. It was the most beautiful coat that the Khan had ever seen.

The Khan thought that if he had on a coat of tiger skin, he would be strong and brave like a tiger. What he did not know was that this coat was made from the magic skin of the King Tiger.

The Khan had a great feast and invited all of his friends. He wanted everyone to see how brave and strong he would be after he put on his new coat.

But when the Khan put on the tiger skin coat, he turned into a tiger. He ran around trying to kill people.

Ku-nan ran up and seized the tiger by the tail. He swung him around his head and hit him on the ground.

That was the end of the Khan who had become a tiger because he put on a coat made from the magic skin of the King Tiger.

Little Han Hsin

Han Hsin lived a long time ago. He was a very small boy. But he could think very well.

One day his ball fell into a hole, and he could not reach it. He sat down by the hole and thought a long time. Then he got a basket and carried dirt to the hole.

Han Hsin put the dirt into the hole and stirred it with a stick. The ball came to the top of the dirt. He put more dirt into the hole. Soon he could reach his ball.

When Han Hsin went to school, he studied hard and always knew his lessons. His teachers all said that he would be a very wise man.

When Han Hsin grew to be a man, he was a very small man. He was no taller than a boy. But he was the wisest man in the kingdom.

In those days every prince had many wise men who lived in his palace. The prince always asked the wise men what to do.

Han Hsin wanted to be one of the wise men at the palace. And so he went to the Prince of Chin Chou.

The Prince of Chin Chou was very big and strong. When he saw little Han Hsin, he laughed and said,

"No man who looks like a little boy can be a wise man. I will not have Han Hsin in my palace."

There was an old wise man in the palace. He went to the Prince and said,

"Do not send this little man away. He is the wisest man in the kingdom. If you send him away, he will go to the prince in the next kingdom. And that prince will overcome your soldiers and take your kingdom."

The Prince of Chin Chou laughed for he was very strong and he had many soldiers.

"I do not believe what you say, old man," said the Prince. "I will send my soldiers after Han Hsin. They will kill him on the mountainside."

The soldiers of the Prince went after Han Hsin. He saw them coming, and he knew that he could not get away. He knew the soldiers were going to kill him.

Han Hsin said to himself,

"I must fool these soldiers of the Prince of Chin Chou. They must not think that I am wise."

Han Hsin lay down on the mountainside with his feet toward the top of the mountain and his head toward the bottom of the mountain. When the soldiers came upon him he looked as if he were sleeping upside down.

The soldiers laughed and laughed. They went back to the palace and told the Prince how silly Han Hsin was sleeping upside down on the mountainside.

The Prince laughed and said to the old wise man,

"Surely such a silly man will never give any trouble to the Prince of Chin Chou."

But the old wise man said,

"Han Hsin is not silly. He is wise for he fooled your soldiers. They thought that he was just a foolish man fast asleep on the mountainside. They laughed at him but did not kill him."

Han Hsin went to the next kingdom. This Prince was making war on the Prince of Chin Chou. He wanted many wise men around him. But he could not see how such a small man could be very wise.

The wise men said to this Prince,

"Make Han Hsin the general of your army and you will win the war against the Prince of Chin Chou."

The Prince believed what his wise men told him. He made little Han Hsin the head of his army. Han Hsin was a very wise general. Soon he became the greatest general in all of China.

The First Kite

Han Hsin was no taller than a boy. But he was very wise. He was the greatest general in all of China.

One time he was at war with the Prince of Chin Chou. The army of the Prince was on the other side of the mountain. It would take a long time for Han Hsin's army to march around the mountain.

Han Hsin said,

"We are going to surprise the army of the Prince of Chin Chou."

Han Hsin ordered his soldiers to make many bags. Han Hsin told the soldiers to fill the bags with dirt.

The soldiers made steps up the mountainside with these bags filled with dirt. Then the army marched over the mountain.

But the Prince of Chin Chou had a very large, strong army. Han Hsin and his men surprised the soldiers, but they did not win the battle.

General Han Hsin had to think of some way to make the soldiers of the Prince of Chin Chou go back to their own kingdom.

At last Han Hsin made a plan. He had his soldiers make a big kite. It was the first kite that had ever been made.

Han Hsin said to his soldiers, "One time the Prince of Chin Chou laughed at me because I was so small. But tonight I will show him how a small man can overcome a big man."

When it was beginning to get dark, Han Hsin had his soldiers tie him to the big kite. Then the soldiers flew the kite up into the sky. They flew the kite over the camp of the soldiers of the Prince of Chin Chou.

When the soldiers saw the big kite up in the sky, they were afraid. They thought some bad dragon from the sky was bringing them misfortune. It was so dark that they could not see Han Hsin tied to the kite.

"Look! Look!" cried the soldiers. "See the bad dragon in the sky."

Then, from out of the sky, the soldiers heard the dragon talking to them.

"Your wives and your sons need you at home. Why don't you go home to them? If you stay here, you will be killed tomorrow."

The soldiers thought a god had spoken to them from the sky. They were afraid. They wanted to see their wives and sons again.

The soldiers talked together and said,

"We do not want to stay here and be killed. We want to go home."

In the darkness of the night, many of the soldiers left the army of the Prince of Chin Chou.

In the morning there were only a few soldiers left. The Prince of Chin Chou knew that he could never win the battle.

And it happened just as the old wise man had said. He had told the Prince of Chin Chou,

"This little man is the wisest man in the Kingdom. And if you send him away, he will go to the prince of the next kingdom and that prince will overcome your soldiers and take your kingdom."

Every year there is kite time in China. The sky is full of kites. There are many kinds of kites. Some look like fish. Some look like dragons. There is also a kite that looks like a man.

This man kite has some words on it which mean,

"Strength of mind is greater than strength of body."

All the boys and girls in China know the story of this kite. They fly this man kite in honor of Han Hsin, the greatest general of China.

The Merchant's Son

There once was a merchant whose name was Wang. He had a very beautiful wife and a fine son. Wang was often away from home to buy goods for his store.

One night when her husband was away, the beautiful wife had a dream. She thought someone was in her room. She woke up and lighted a lantern. She looked all over the room but found no one. Just as she was getting back to sleep again, she saw a fox run out of the door.

The next morning Mrs. Wang called her servant,

"Go and tell my son, Hu, that he must come to me. I am very sick. I am afraid that I am going to die."

The son came at once to his mother. He found her very sick.

"I will go and get a doctor," said Hu.

"No," said his mother. "I am afraid a doctor cannot help me."

That night Hu and the servant stayed in the room with Mrs. Wang. In the middle of the night, they went to sleep. In the morning, Mrs. Wang was gone.

The servant was afraid. But Hu went through the house looking for his mother.

He found his mother in another room fast asleep. When she awoke, she did not know where she was. She did not know her son. And she did not know her servant.

The servant and Hu got Mrs. Wang back into her own room. She kept talking as if she were dreaming. Hu heard her say,

"Make the fox go away. Make the fox go away."

Then Hu remembered the stories about the Magic Fox that his grandfather had told him.

The Magic Fox can change himself into a man, but he must always keep his foxtail. The Magic Fox can hurt people and make them sick.

Hu went to the kitchen and got a big sharp knife. He lighted a lantern and sat beside his mother. In the middle of the night, Mrs. Wang began talking.

"Make the fox go away. He is going to kill me."

Hu stood up. Something that looked like a fox ran from the door. Hu brought his big knife down and cut off the end of the fox's tail.

"That old fox will not come here again tonight," said Hu. He took the end of the foxtail and put it in his pocket. Then he went to sleep.

The next morning Hu found drops of blood in the garden and on the garden wall. He followed the drops of blood. Soon he was in the garden of the Ho family. Hu did not know what to do next, so he went home.

That evening Mr. Wang came home from his journey. His wife did not know him. When Hu told him the story of the fox, Mr. Wang sent at once for a doctor.

The doctor gave Mrs. Wang medicine and said many magic words. But Mrs. Wang did not get any better.

One evening, Hu hid in the garden of the Ho family. He heard some men talking. He looked from behind the bushes and saw two men drinking wine. A servant in a long brown coat kept filling their cups with wine.

"Get us some white wine for tomorrow night," said one of the men to the servant.

When the two men went away, the servant took off his long brown coat.

Hu watched the servant. He saw that he had two arms and two legs just like a man. But he had a big foxtail that lay over his back.

Hu was afraid to move. He hid behind the bushes until the sun came up. Then the servant got up and went through the grass. And Hu ran home as fast as he could.

The Magic Foxes

Mr. Wang, the merchant, had to go into town. Hu, his son, wanted to go with him. So the two of them went off to town after telling the servant to take good care of Mrs. Wang who was sick.

When they got to town Hu saw a long foxtail hanging in the window of a shop.

"Please, Father," said Hu, "please buy me that foxtail."

Mr. Wang went into the shop and bought the foxtail. He gave it to Hu, who put it inside his coat.

"And now, Father, I will need some money for there is something I must buy," said Hu.

Mr. Wang gave Hu some money and went off to his store. Hu went at once to the wine shop. He bought some white wine.

"I will come for this wine before I go home," said Hu to the wine merchant.

Then Hu went to see his aunt who lived in the town.

"My mother has been very sick," said Hu. "She is better now. But a big rat is in the house. Mother wants to kill it because it has eaten a hole in her dress."

"I will give you some poison so that your mother can kill that rat," said his aunt.

She gave Hu some poison which he put in his pocket.

"Thank you, my dear aunt," said Hu.

Hu went off to the wine shop as fast as he could go. When the wine merchant was not looking, he put the poison in the white wine which he had bought. Then he went off to the market place.

Hu looked and looked at the people in the market place. Soon he saw the servant whom he had seen in the Ho family garden.

Hu followed the servant and said,

"I have been looking for you."

The servant was very surprised and said,

"Why should you be looking for me? I do not know you. Where do you live?"

"I live in a hole on the side of the hill. Our family has lived there a long time, the same as yours."

"What is your name?" asked the servant.

"My name is Hu, and I saw you with the two men in the Ho family garden."

The servant did not know what to think.

Hu opened his coat and showed the servant the end of the foxtail that his father had bought for him that morning.

"We can be men sometimes," said Hu, "but we must always carry this with us."

"What are you doing in town?" asked the servant.

"I am buying white wine for my father," said Hu.

"That is the very thing that I must get for my masters," said the servant. "But I will have to steal it for I have no money."

"Who are your masters?" asked Hu. "I would like to know them for we are all of one family."

"My masters are two brothers," said the servant. "They come every night and drink wine in the garden of the Ho family. They tell stories of what they have done for they have much magic.

"One of my masters has put a spell on the beautiful wife of the merchant Wang. The son of the lady cut off the end of my master's tail, and he is very angry. The beautiful lady will die very soon."

"Your masters must have the white wine or they will be angry with you," said Hu.

"Yes," said the servant. "But I will have to steal it."

"I bought some white wine at the wine shop," said Hu. "I was going to get it before I went home. I will give it to you for I have money to buy some more wine, and we are all of one family."

The servant in the long brown coat went with Hu to the wine shop. The wine merchant gave Hu the white wine he had bought. Hu gave it to the servant.

That night Mrs. Wang slept very quietly. She did not dream that a fox was trying to kill her.

In the morning, Hu told his father the story of the men he had seen in the Ho family garden.

"They had fox tails," said Hu. "And I knew they were magic foxes who had changed themselves into men. Yesterday in town I met the servant who wanted some white wine. I showed him the foxtail that you had bought for me. I made him believe that I was a magic fox too. And I gave him some poisoned wine."

Hu and his father went as fast as they could to the Ho family garden. There in the grass they found three dead foxes and beside them the jar of white wine.

"Why did you not tell me about the foxes?" asked Mr. Wang.

"I was afraid the foxes would know," said Hu. "I did not tell anyone what I was going to do."

The beautiful Mrs. Wang got well. And Mr. and Mrs. Wang were very proud of their son Hu who killed the magic foxes.

Ma Tsai and the Landlord

It was time for the Landlord to come and get the rent. The Landlord was a greedy man and took almost all of the grain for his rent.

Ma Tsai thought to himself, "My father and my mother worked all of their lives on this farm. They never had enough to eat because the Landlord took so much grain. And now I have a good harvest but the Landlord still comes and takes it. I will fool that greedy Landlord."

Ma Tsai took some of his grain and gave it to a hunter. The hunter gave Ma Tsai two live foxes. Then Ma Tsai took some of his grain and bought many fat hens. He put the hens in the henhouse.

Ma Tsai hid one fox inside the house. But he tied a rope around the neck of the other fox and took it everywhere he went.

One day the Landlord came to get his rent. He saw Ma Tsai in the field.

"Ma Tsai," called the Landlord, "is your grain ready for your rent?"

"Yes," said Ma Tsai. "I have had a good harvest and the grain is ready for you."

"I will come and get it tomorrow," said the Landlord.

Then the Landlord saw the fox on the end of the rope.

"What are you doing with a fox on the end of a rope?" asked the Landlord. "You had better kill it or it will get away."

"This fox is my pet," said Ma Tsai. "It brings me nice fat chickens to eat."

Then Ma Tsai said to the fox, "Go, my little pet, and bring me some nice fat chickens."

Ma Tsai took the rope off of the fox. It ran away as fast as it could go.

The Landlord was very much surprised. He had never heard of a pet fox that would catch chickens and bring them to its master.

"Come and have dinner with me tomorrow," said Ma Tsai. "I will show you what fine fat chickens my little pet brings to me. We will have a feast tomorrow."

The Landlord came to dinner. He had never seen such a feast of fine fat chickens. The chickens had been cooked in many ways.

The greedy Landlord ate and ate and ate. He thought that this pet fox would be a wonderful thing to have. Then he could have chicken every day.

At last he said to Ma Tsai, "Where is the fox that brought you all of these fine chickens?"

"My little pet is sleeping. He is very tired after being up all night," said Ma Tsai.

"Bring him out," said the Landlord. "I wish to see him."

Ma Tsai went to the room where he had hidden the other fox. He tied a rope around its neck and took it to the Landlord.

As soon as the Landlord saw the fox, he knew that he must have it.

"That is a fine fox," said the Landlord. "Will you take a hundred pieces of silver for your pet fox?"

"Oh, no!" cried Ma Tsai. "I will never be hungry as long as my pet fox is with me. You can take my grain for the rent but I could not sell my pet fox."

"I do not want your grain," said the Landlord. "I want your pet fox. Will you sell him to me for two hundred pieces of silver?"

Ma Tsai looked very sad, but he laughed to himself as he said,

"If you want my pet fox, I guess I must sell him to you. But I would have to have three hundred pieces of silver for him."

The Landlord paid the money and took the pet fox home. He was so glad to get the fox that he did not take any of the grain for his rent.

When the Landlord got home, he said to his wife,

"I have brought home the most wonderful fox. It will get us all the fat chickens that we can eat."

The wife laughed and said, "You are a very foolish man."

"Wait and see," said the Landlord. "My little pet, go and get me some fat chickens."

The Landlord took the rope off of the fox. The fox ran away as fast as he could go.

The Landlord waited all day for the fox to come back with a fat chicken.

The Landlord waited all the next day for the fox to come back.

The third day the Landlord knew that he had been fooled by Ma Tsai.

His wife laughed at him and called him a foolish man.

The greedy Landlord never told anyone about the fox that he had bought from Ma Tsai. He did not want anyone to know that he had been a foolish man.

The Prince of Peking

There once was an old Emperor who had two sons. The Empress, or wife of the Emperor, wanted the oldest son to rule the kingdom after the Emperor died.

But the people all loved the younger son the best. The Empress was afraid that the Emperor might listen to the people and make the younger son the ruler.

The Empress went to the Emperor and said,

"My dear husband, I think that you should send your younger son away to the Kingdom of Yen."

The Emperor loved his younger son very much. But he could see that it might be best for him to give his younger son a kingdom of his own.

The young Prince got ready for the journey to the Kingdom of Yen. Before he left, his old teacher came to him and said,

"My son, I am sorry to see you go away from your father's kingdom. You are going into a new country, and I cannot go with you."

"I shall never forget you," said the Prince, "and I will try to remember what you have told me."

The old teacher gave the Prince a letter.

"Take this magic letter. Do not open it unless you are in great trouble. Then open it and read the first thing that your eyes see. This letter will help you out of any trouble."

The Prince thanked his old teacher and went on his way. He went to the Kingdom of Yen.

The Prince was not happy, for the Kingdom of Yen was not beautiful. There were no trees and flowers, only stones and mud. There were no cities of beautiful houses, only huts.

The Prince sat upon a stone. He was very sad. He thought of the beautiful palace where he had lived all of his life. He thought of his old father and he knew that he would never see him again. The Prince knew that he must stay in the Kingdom of Yen.

As the Prince was sitting on the stone, he thought of the letter that his old teacher had given him. He took the magic letter out of his pocket and opened it. This is what he read:

"Build a beautiful city. The plan for the city of Peking is on the back of this paper."

The Prince built the city of Peking and made it one of the most beautiful cities in China.

This happened a very long time ago. The name Peking has been changed to Peiping. But Peiping is still one of the biggest and one of the most beautiful cities of China.

Water for Peking

The people were happy in the beautiful city of Peking. But one day the ministers came to the Prince of Peking and said,

"The people are crying in the streets because the wells have dried up. There is no water. What will the people do without water?"

The Prince did not know that a dragon and his wife lived in a cave outside the wall of the city of Peking. The dragons had lived there for thousands and thousands of years.

The He-dragon and the She-dragon did not mind if people built a city near their cave. But when some men took the stones from their cave to fix the wall of the city, the dragon and his wife got very angry.

"My husband," said the She-dragon, "we have lived in our cave for a long, long time. But now the Prince of Peking has hurt our cave, and we must go away."

"If we go away, we will take all the water from the wells of Peking with us in our magic baskets," said the He-dragon.

"Let us change ourselves into an old man and an old woman," said the She-dragon. "We will go to the Prince in a dream and ask him if we may fill our baskets with water."

"The Prince will tell us we can take the water," said the He-dragon. "Because he gave us the water, he cannot tell us to bring it back."

The He-dragon and the She-dragon went to the Prince in a dream. The Prince did not know that the old man and the old woman had great magic.

In the Prince's dream, the old man and the old woman asked the Prince if they could go away from the city of Peking and take with them their baskets filled with water. The Prince told them to take the water and go.

The next morning the ministers came to the Prince and told him there was no water in the wells of Peking.

In his trouble, the Prince remembered the magic letter. He opened it and read the story of the He-dragon and the She-dragon who had changed themselves into an old man and an old woman.

The Prince also read in the magic letter just how he was to get the water back to the city of Peking.

The Prince called to his servants to bring his armor and his spear. He called to his servants to bring his horse. He put on his armor and got on his horse. Then, with his spear in his hand, he rode out of the city of Peking.

The Prince rode like the wind. Soon he came to an old man and an old woman. The old woman was pulling a cart along the road. The old man was pushing the cart from behind.

The Prince saw in the cart the two baskets that he had seen in his dream.

The Prince rode up to the cart and put his spear through one of the baskets. Out of the basket came a river of water. The Prince turned his horse and rode away as fast as he could go, but the water came roaring after him.

The Prince rode his horse up a hill. When he looked down from the hill he could see a river of water going down the countryside. The Prince knew that the people who lived in the city of Peking would always have water.

The Prince rode down the hill and back to the city of Peking. He had carried out the plan that he had read in the magic letter that his old master had given him. And the city of Peking had water.

The King of the Monkeys

On the side of a very high mountain, there was a rocky point. On the very top of this rocky point was a rock that looked like a stone monkey.

The Emperor of Heaven looked down and saw the stone monkey.

"I will give that stone monkey life. Then he can run over the mountainside," said the Emperor of Heaven.

So the stone monkey became a live monkey and played on the mountainside.

The monkey went down the mountain to where the trees grew. He met the monkeys that lived in the trees. He soon became King of the Monkeys.

The King of the Monkeys dressed in beautiful silks. He had gold chains around his neck. He was called Sun Hou-Tzu, which means the monkey-that-knows-all.

Sun Hou-Tzu could go anywhere in the world. One day he went under the sea to visit the Dragon King.

The Dragon King had a beautiful palace under the sea. He had many jewels and silk coats.

"What is the most wonderful thing that you own?" asked Sun Hou-Tzu.

"It is this little rod," said the Dragon King. "It can make a ladder to heaven or it can become so small that I can carry it behind my ear. This magic rod makes all my wishes come true."

"I must have that rod!" cried Sun Hou-Tzu. And he snatched the rod from the Dragon King's hand and ran out of the palace.

The Dragon King was very angry and sent his servants after the monkey. But Sun Hou-Tzu got back to his trees.

Sun Hou-Tzu built a beautiful palace. He gave great parties and invited kings and princes.

Sun Hou-Tzu had the magic rod, and he could change himself into anything he wanted to be.

Most of all, Sun Hou-Tzu wanted to be an Immortal and never die. But the magic rod could not make the monkey an Immortal.

Sun Hou-Tzu heard the story of the magic peach tree that grew in the garden of the Western Empress whose name was Wang Mu.

The peach tree gave fruit only once in every thousand years.

The peaches were very large. Whoever ate one of the magic peaches would never die.

When the peaches were ripe, Wang Mu gave a party called the Peach Festival. All the Immortals came to eat the magic peaches.

Now it was time for the Peach Festival. Sun Hou-Tzu went to the garden.

When the King of the Monkeys got to the garden of Wang Mu, he put all the servants to sleep with his magic rod. Then he ate a peach. Now Sun Hou-Tzu was an Immortal and would never die.

The Lord of Heaven

The Emperor of Heaven was sorry that he had made the stone monkey into a live monkey. The monkey had made nothing but trouble in the world. Because he had eaten the magic peach, he was an Immortal and would never die.

The Emperor of Heaven went to the great Lord of Heaven and said,

"Please do something about the bad monkey named Sun Hou-Tzu."

The Lord of Heaven said,

"Go and tell this monkey that I wish to have a talk with him."

Sun Hou-Tzu came to the Lord of Heaven who said,

"What is your greatest wish?"

"I wish to be a god and live in the heavens," said Sun Hou-Tzu.

"What makes you think that you can be a god in heaven?" asked the Lord of Heaven.

"I have eaten the magic peach. Now I am an Immortal, and I will never die," said Sun Hou-Tzu. "I can go up in the heavens and down in the sea. I can go anywhere I want."

The Lord of Heaven picked up Sun Hou-Tzu and said,

"If you can leave my hand, I will let you be a god in heaven."

Sun Hou-Tzu gave a big jump. He went to the ends of the earth. He wrote his name on one of the five pillars at the ends of the earth to show that he had been there. Then, with a big jump, he was back before the great Lord of Heaven.

The Lord of Heaven held up his hand. There, written on one of his fingers, was the name that Sun Hou-Tzu had put on the pillar at the ends of the earth.

"Don't you know, silly monkey, that all the world is in my hand? The Lord of Heaven is over all."

The Lord of Heaven shut Sun Hou-Tzu in the middle of five high mountains. Even the magic rod could not get the King of the Monkeys out of the mountains.

Sun Hou-Tzu stayed in the mountains a long time. But one day Sun Hou-Tzu began to pray to the Goddess of Mercy.

"Please, help me. Show me how I can become a good monkey. I will try to help the people on earth."

Sun Hou-Tzu prayed every day. The Goddess of Mercy heard him. She went to the Lord of Heaven and said,

"Great Lord of Heaven, Sun Hou-Tzu is sorry for all the trouble he has made. He wants to learn to be a good monkey and to help the people on earth."

The Lord of Heaven thought a long time. Then he said,

"There is a holy man who is going on a long journey. I will let Sun Hou-Tzu go with him as his servant. This holy man can teach the monkey to be good."

Sun Hou-Tzu became a servant to the holy man. At first the monkey did not know how to be good.

Many times Sun Hou-Tzu made trouble for his master. So the holy man put a "head-splitting helmet" on Sun Hou-Tzu's head. Sun Hou-Tzu looked very funny. But whenever the monkey wanted to do something bad, the helmet would hurt his head.

Sun Hou-Tzu became a good servant. He took care of his master. He used his magic rod to help others.

Sun Hou-Tzu could change himself into anything he wanted to be. This helped him overcome bad demons who would have hurt his master.

The journey with the holy man lasted many years. There are many stories about what Sun Hou-Tzu and his master did on their journey. But, at last, they got safely home. They are now with the great Lord of Heaven and the Immortals.

The Yellow Dragon

Wu was the son of a farmer named Yin. His mother had died when he was very young. His old grandmother took care of him.

Wu loved the flowers and the birds. He liked to watch the clouds in the sky and he dreamed many dreams. His old grandmother told him many stories about dragons that lived in the sky and about the spirits from Heaven that sometimes came upon the earth.

One day when Wu was about fourteen years old he was sitting by the garden gate watching the clouds. Suddenly he saw a young man on a white horse coming down the road. Four servants were with him. One of the servants held an umbrella over the young man so that the sun would not burn him.

The young man stopped his horse at the garden gate and said to Wu,

"Son of Yin, I am tired. May I enter your father's house and rest for a time?"

"Enter," said Wu. "My father will be honored to have you rest in his house."

Wu called his father. The farmer and the young man talked together. Food was brought and the young man ate.

But Wu just sat and did not say a word. He watched the young man and his servants.

When the young man was ready to go, the servants brought his white horse. The young man got on his horse and then he said to Wu,

"Good-by! I shall come again."

Wu bowed low and said,

"Come! I shall be glad to see you again."

Then Wu saw that the servant turned the umbrella upside down as he went through the garden gate.

That evening the farmer said,

"The young man knew my name was Yin. I wonder who he was for I have never seen him before."

"He was a very strange young man," said Wu. "He did not walk upon the ground. And his white horse had spots of five colors."

Yin, the farmer, was very much afraid, and he said,

"It is only spirits that do not need to walk upon the ground. We must go and ask your old grandmother what this means."

"Grandmother," said Wu, "the young man and his white horse did not walk upon the ground. And when the servant went out of the garden gate, he turned the umbrella upside down.

"I watched the young man on his white horse go down the road. Pretty soon I saw the young man and his four servants go up into the clouds."

The old Grandmother closed her eyes and then she said,

"The white horse spotted with the five colors is a dragon horse. And the young man is the Yellow Dragon. He has gone up into the clouds to make a storm. There is going to be a great storm for he had his four servants with him."

"Why did the servant turn the umbrella upside down when he went out of our garden gate?" asked Yin.

"That was a good sign," said the old Grandmother. "When the storm comes, the Yellow Dragon will not let our house be hurt. I must go to sleep now for I am very tired."

But Wu and his father, Yin, did not go to sleep. Wu put on a yellow robe that his grandmother had made him. In the middle of the night it began to rain.

It rained and it rained. Never had there been such a great rain.

In the morning, Yin looked out of the window. There was a lake of water all around the house.

"Our house is going to be washed away," said Yin.

"No," said Wu. "The Yellow Dragon will not let the rain hurt us. Remember that the servant turned the umbrella upside down when he went out of our gate."

"The water is coming down the sides of the mountain," said Yin. "The river is covering the land. The people of the village will be drowned."

"Listen, my honored father," said Wu, "there is no rain falling on our house."

"Some great magic is keeping us safe," said Yin.

In the middle of the next day, the rain stopped and the sun came out. Wu went and stood by the garden gate. He looked up into the sky and he thought he saw the Yellow Dragon.

The Yellow Dragon called to him,

"Wu, son of Yin the farmer, when you are a man you are going to wear a yellow robe. You are going to be a man of magic. And you will live in the palace of the Emperor."

And it happened just as the Yellow Dragon said that it would.

The House of Chang Kung

Long, long ago there lived a very kind man named Chang Kung. He had a great family house with a wall around it. There were many courtyards within this wall. And many rooms opened on these courtyards.

The wives and children of Chang Kung's sons lived happily in the family house. The wives and children of his grandsons lived happily there, too. There were more than a hundred people in Chang Kung's family.

There were a hundred dogs that lived in the courtyards of Chang Kung's family house. The dogs did not fight. They wagged their tails. There was nothing but happiness in Chang Kung's family house.

Everyone in the country talked about Chang Kung's House of Happiness. At last the Emperor heard about it.

"Happiness is what I want most of all," said the Emperor to himself. "I will go and visit Chang Kung and ask him how to make my beautiful palace a House of Happiness."

The Emperor made ready to visit Chang Kung. He was carried in a golden sedan chair with curtains of yellow silk. The soldiers of the Emperor marched in front. The mandarins and ministers followed the sedan chair. There never had been so many visitors at Chang Kung's house.

Chang Kung was very old, but he bowed to the ground before the Emperor. The Emperor said, "Most excellent and aged sir, we have heard that your family house is a House of Happiness. No cross word is ever spoken. Can this be true?"

"Son of Heaven," said Chang Kung, "my poor house is honored by your visit. No cross words are spoken here, for kind words please the gods. Will you walk in my courtyards and meet my family?"

The Emperor walked in the courtyards of Chang Kung's family house. He met the sons and the grandsons. He saw the wives and the children. He saw the dogs wagging their tails. He saw nothing but happiness.

Then the Emperor and the mandarins went to Chang Kung's Hall of Politeness.

The Emperor said to Chang Kung,

"Most excellent and aged sir, I should like to know your secret of happiness."

Chang Kung told the servants to bring him the ink and the brush and a tablet of wood on which to write. Then Chang Kung sat and wrote one hundred words on the piece of wood.

Chang Kung bowed low before the Emperor and gave him the tablet of wood.

"Son of Heaven, I give you my secret of happiness."

The Emperor looked at the tablet in surprise.

"You have written one hundred words, and yet you have written only one word."

"Son of Heaven," said Chang Kung, bowing low to the Emperor, "there is only one word to my secret of happiness. That word is 'kindness.'"

The Emperor was so pleased that he took the brush and wrote on a large tablet of wood the story of the House of Happiness. He told Chang Kung to put this tablet over the door to his family house.

People from all over the country came to read the Emperor's story of the House of Happiness.

The good and kind Chang Kung, whose family house was called the House of Happiness, was made an Immortal by the Gods of Heaven. He is called the Kitchen God. His picture is put above the stove in the kitchen.

The children know that he watches them. There will be happiness in the house if people are good and kind.

The Peacock Maidens

There once was a king who had
a brave son named Chaushutun.
Chaushutun had a magic bow that
he had found in a well. An arrow
shot from this magic bow always
found its mark. No one but
Chaushutun was strong enough to
pull the magic bow.

The King and Queen wanted
their son to marry. But Chaushutun
found that he could not love any
of the beautiful girls of the court.

Chaushutun was very unhappy.
He said to his father and mother,

"I must ride over the plains and over the mountains. I will take my magic bow and arrows. I will find a princess whom I can love."

For a year and a day Chaushutun rode over the plains and over the mountains. At last he met an old hunter. Chaushutun and the old hunter went hunting.

The old hunter said,

"I have never met a young man whose arrow always finds its mark."

"Hunting brings me no happiness," said Chaushutun.

"Why are you so sad?" asked the old hunter.

"I ride over the plains and over the mountains for I want to find a wife whom I may love," said Chaushutun.

The old hunter thought for a long time. Then he said,

"Tonight I will take you to a lake where you will see seven beautiful princesses dancing on the sand."

That night Chaushutun and the old hunter hid behind some bushes by the lake. They waited until the moon was high in the heavens. Then they saw seven peacocks come down to the shore of the lake.

The peacocks took off their coats of beautiful feathers. Chaushutun was surprised to see seven beautiful maidens dancing in the moonlight. The youngest maiden was the most beautiful.

As the maidens danced, one by one they put on their coats of beautiful feathers. Chaushutun saw seven peacocks fly away.

"It is the youngest maiden whom I love," said Chaushutun. "How can I ever see her again?"

"Do not be so sad," said the old hunter. "In seven days the Peacock Maidens will come again and dance on the sand."

"But seven days is a long, long time," said Chaushutun.

For seven days Chaushutun waited for the Peacock Maidens to come back to the lake. While he was waiting, he cut a branch from a tree and made a long hook.

Chaushutun and the old hunter were waiting behind the bushes when the seven peacocks flew down to the lake. Chaushutun had his long hook with him. While the Peacock Maidens were dancing, he took his hook and drew the peacock coat of the youngest princess into the bushes.

It was time for the Peacock
Maidens to fly away.

"I cannot find my peacock coat,"
said Namarona, the youngest
princess. She started to cry.

"Do not cry," said Chaushutun.
"I wanted you to stay here." He
came out from behind the bush
and walked on the shore.

The girls were so afraid when
they heard a man's voice that six
of them put on their peacock
coats and flew away. But Namarona
stood and looked at the handsome
prince.

Chaushutun bowed low and gave
the princess her peacock coat.

The Prince and the Princess sat on the sand by the lake and talked a long time. When the Prince asked the Princess to be his wife, she said that she would, for she loved him very much.

"I will put my peacock coat around us and we will fly to your father's kingdom," said Namarona.

Chaushutun and Namarona told the old hunter good-by. Then off they flew into the sky. They went back to the kingdom where the Prince's father ruled.

The Bad Mahashena

The King and Queen were happy to see their son again. They loved beautiful Namarona, the Peacock Princess, as soon as they saw her.

But there was one person in the palace who did not like Namarona. This was Mahashena, the minister to the King.

Mahashena said to the King, "Where did the Peacock Princess come from? Who is her father? Who is her mother? How do you know that she is not a witch?"

The King did not know what to say to his minister.

Everything was being made ready for the wedding of the Prince and the Peacock Princess. Then news came that an army was marching toward the kingdom.

Prince Chaushutun went to his father and said,

"I must go and lead our soldiers against this army. When I come back, I will marry the Peacock Princess. Take good care of her while I am gone."

As soon as the Prince had left, the bad Mahashena began to tell lies to the King.

"Our soldiers are being killed by the army marching against your kingdom. Your kingdom will be taken from you unless you kill the Peacock Princess. She is a witch."

Every day Mahashena brought news that the King's soldiers were being killed. The King was afraid that his son would be killed, too. The King was afraid for his kingdom.

So the King said,

"We do not know this Peacock Princess. We must kill her, for she is a witch. Tomorrow she must die."

The Queen was very unhappy. She loved the Peacock Princess, but she could do nothing to save her. She helped to dress Namarona in her most beautiful clothes.

Namarona was not afraid to die, but tears were in her eyes. She cried because she had to leave Chaushutun for she loved him.

The guards took Namarona before the King. Bowing low, she said,

"I am not afraid to die. I only ask that you give me my peacock coat and let me dance once more before I die."

The King looked at the Peacock Princess, and he said to the guards,

"Bring her peacock coat and let her dance for she is very beautiful."

The Princess put on her peacock coat. She danced as she had never danced before.

There were tears in the eyes of all the people watching, for the Princess was too young and too beautiful to die. Faster and faster Namarona danced. Then, with a cry, she put her peacock coat around her and flew up into the sky.

"Catch her! Catch her!" cried the bad Mahashena. But the beautiful peacock flew away.

A messenger came riding up to the King.

"Prince Chaushutun, the leader of your brave soldiers, has driven the enemy from your kingdom. He rides home as fast as he can and wishes his wedding to take place at once."

Then the King knew that the bad minister had been telling him lies. He pointed to Mahashena and said to the guards,

"Take that bad man away and kill him!"

When Prince Chaushutun came home and found that Namarona was gone, he got on his horse and rode away, taking his magic bow and arrows with him.

"I shall never come home until I have found my Peacock Princess," cried Prince Chaushutun.

The Peacock Dance

Prince Chaushutun rode over the plains and over the mountains. At last he came to the lake where he had first seen his Peacock Princess. The old hunter was waiting for him.

"The Peacock Princess left this bracelet for you," said the old hunter. "She knew that you would come back to the lake."

Chaushutun put the bracelet on his arm. "I must find her," cried the Prince. "Where has she gone?"

"She has gone to her father's kingdom," said the old hunter. "You will have to go on a long and hard road before you will see your Peacock Princess again."

The old hunter called to a monkey in the trees. The monkey came down out of the trees and showed Chaushutun the way.

Day and night, the monkey and the Prince went on their way. At last they came to a river. There was no bridge. Chaushutun did not know how to get across the river. He walked along the rocks, but he could find no way of getting across.

The monkey called and called. A great snake came out of the water. The great snake coiled its tail around a big rock on one side of the river. Then the great snake stretched itself across the river. It coiled its head around a rock on the other side of the river.

The monkey and Chaushutun walked across the river on the snake's back.

Chaushutun and the monkey went on and on over plains and over mountains. At last they were so tired that they could not go on.

"You must go on alone," said the monkey. "I am too tired."

Chaushutun sat under a big tree. In the tree lived the two biggest birds in the world. Chaushutun heard these birds talking.

"We must go to the King's feast tomorrow," said one bird.

"It will be a great feast," said the other bird. "The seventh daughter of the King has come home. She has been away a long time."

"These big birds are going to fly to the kingdom where Namarona lives. They must take me with them," thought Chaushutun.

When the big birds were fast asleep, Chaushutun climbed the tree. He hid under the wings of one of the birds, and tied himself to a big feather. In the morning when the birds flew away, one of them carried Chaushutun to the kingdom where Namarona lived.

The big birds sat upon a tree by the palace.

"I do not feel well," said one of the birds. "I feel so heavy."

The big bird shook his feathers, and Chaushutun dropped out of the tree. He was in the garden of the palace.

There was a fountain in the garden. As Chaushutun watched, five beautiful girls came to get water from the fountain. One by one the girls filled their jars with water and went into the palace. When the last girl had filled her jar, Chaushutun stepped out from behind a bush and spoke to her.

"I pray that you tell me if your mistress is as beautiful as you are."

The girl smiled and said,

"My mistress is Namarona, the youngest and most beautiful daughter of the King. She has come back to the palace.

"There is to be a big feast because everyone is happy that she is home again. But my mistress does not seem happy. She sits by her window and cries."

Chaushutun dropped Namarona's bracelet into the jar of water and said,

"Tell your mistress that this water will wash her tears away and she will smile again."

The girl carried the jar of water into the palace to the room where Namarona sat and thought of Chaushutun. As the girl poured the water out for the bath, Namarona saw her bracelet.

"Where did you get that bracelet?" cried Namarona.

"Perhaps the young man put it into my jar," said the girl. "He was by the fountain, and he told me to tell you that this water would wash away your tears and you would smile again."

"He is here!" cried Namarona. "Chaushutun has come for me. Get my most beautiful dress. I must take him to my father."

But the King's soldiers had found Chaushutun in the palace garden. They had already taken him to the King.

"Are you the young man who stole my youngest daughter?" asked the King.

"I love Namarona very much, and I want her to be my wife," said Chaushutun.

The King looked at Chaushutun for a long time. He was a fine young man. But the King wanted to be sure that he loved Namarona.

"I have seven daughters," said the King. "In a dark room you will see seven hands by the light on one small lantern. If you can pick Namarona's hand, then I will know that you love her."

That night Chaushutun stood before a black curtain. There were seven holes in the curtain. Through the holes, Chaushutun saw seven white hands. He did not know what to do.

Then a firefly flew into the room. The firefly sat upon one of the white hands. At once Chaushutun knew that this was the hand of Namarona.

He took the white hand in his and said,

"This is the hand of the Princess Namarona whom I love very much."

"Yes," said the King, "that is the hand of Namarona. Now we will have the wedding feast."

Namarona and Chaushutun were very happy. The wedding feast lasted many days. The seven princesses put on their peacock coats and danced the Peacock Dance.

Even today beautiful girls dance the Peacock Dance to bring them happiness.

How to Say Some
Chinese Words

Chang Kung	chahng-kung
Chaushutun	chu-shoo'-tun
China	chi-nah
Chin Chou	chin-choh
Chinese	chi-neez'
dragon	drag'-un
Emperor	ehm'-per-er
Empress	ehm'-prehs
Han Hsin	hahn-shi-en
Ho	ho
Hu	hoo
Immortal	i-mor'-tl
Khan	khan
Kingdom of Yen	king-dum uv yehn
Ku-nan	koo-nahn
Ma Liang	mah-layng
Mandarin	mahn-da-rin
Ma Tsai	mah-tsi
Namarona	nahm-a-ronah
Peking	pee-king
Sun Hou Tzu	sun-hoo-tsu
Wang	wahng
Wang Mu	wahng-moo
Wu	woo
Yin	yin
Yurt	yurt